# The Wonderfu World of Willow

## Willow and CocoPops Series (Book 1)

Written by Rachel McGrath

Illustrated by Mario Tereso

The Wonderful World of Willow © *2015 Rachel McGrath*

Illustrations and Cover Design by Mario Tereso.

All other images (foreground) © 2015 Rachel McGrath
www.rachelmcgrath.net
Published by McGrath House

ISBN-13: *978-1517697334*
ISBN-10: *1517697336*

Dedicated to **Benjamin Weston**, my fabulous, cheeky, gorgeous Godson who has just turned two years old!

1

Meet Willow!

Willow is a girl cat!

Willow lives in a wonderful world!

3

Willow has long, fluffy fur filled with lots of different colours.

Her fur is ginger, brown, black and white.

Willow is a pretty cat!

Willow is six years old.

In cat years that means she is an adult!

But, Willow still enjoys chasing toys and playing games.

Willow is a playful cat!

When Willow is hungry she meows.

She loves to eat fresh meat.

Willow's favourite food is chicken.

Willow is a greedy cat!

Willow loves her house by the canal.

During the day she explores the gardens, or she sits by the water watching the ducks and the geese.

Willow is a happy cat!

Willow loves the sunshine.

Willow stays in the garden all day long, stretching out in the sunshine.

Sometimes she sleeps all day.

Willow is a lazy cat!

Willow can jump very high.

Willow climbs very tall trees so that she can get close to the birds.

She sits very still and hopes that the birds will not see her.

Willow is a clever cat.

Willow loves watching the birds.

Sometimes she watches the birds for hours.

But the birds see her and they quickly fly away.

Willow cannot fly.

Willow also likes to watch the ducks and the geese as they swim in the canal.

She sits by the edge of the water watching them all day long.

Sometimes she gets very close to the water, but Willow cannot swim.

There are other animals that live near the canal.

There are dogs and cats that like to play.

Willow says hello to the other animals by the canal.

Willow has lots of friends.

There is a big grey cat that lives near the canal.

Willow is afraid of the grey cat.

When she sees him she will hiss and spit.

Willow does not like the big grey cat!

Sometimes the big grey cat chases Willow.

Willow runs away from the big grey cat through the gardens and along the canal.

Willow is a fast cat!

25

Willow uses her cat flap to hide from the big grey cat inside her house.

Willow can go inside or outside whenever she pleases using her cat flap.

Willow is a scaredy cat.

27

Willow likes her cat flap.

She can go inside her house or outside to the garden whenever she pleases.

Willow is a lucky cat.

When it is cold Willow likes to stay inside the house.

She likes to sleep by the fire.

Willow likes to stay warm when the nights are cold.

Willow is a house cat.

Willow loves to be cuddled.

She enjoys sitting on laps with her fur being stroked.

Willow purrs when she is happy.

Willow is a friendly cat!

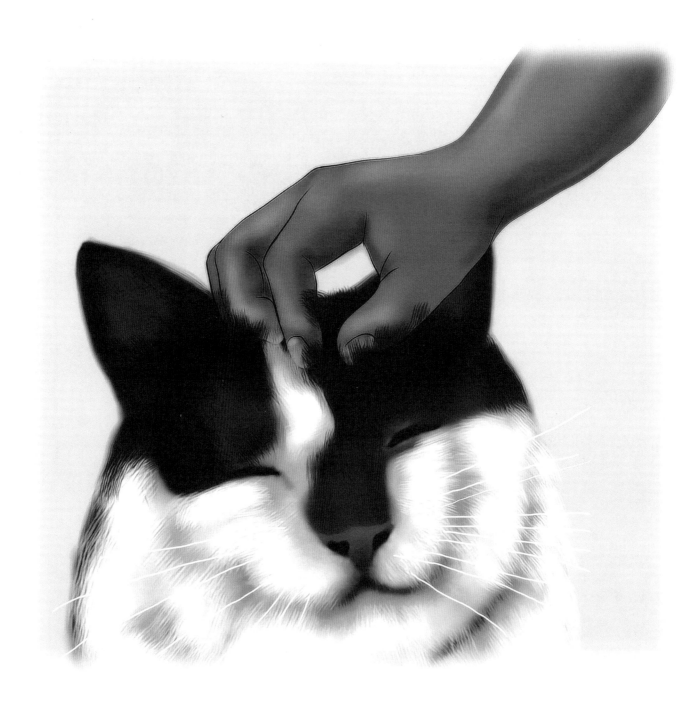

33

Willow is happiest when she is being scratched between the ears.

She purrs and meows with happiness.

Willow is a spoilt cat!

At night, Willow likes to sleep on the end of the bed.

She stretches herself out, taking up lots of space, and she purrs.

Willow is a sleepy cat!

37

Willow lives in a wonderful world where she has lots of adventures!

Willow is the luckiest cat in the world!

## About Willow

Willow is a lovely girl cat, living in Kings Langley, Hertfordshire.
This is her story, and there will be many more.
If you enjoyed this story, Willow would love you to write a review on Amazon,
Goodreads, Barnes and Noble or wherever you purchased this book.
Reviews are important and helpful.
Thank you!

The Wonderful World of Willow

Rachel McGrath

Proof

Made in the USA
Charleston, SC
13 October 2015